PUFFIN BOOKS
SHIVAJI

Sonia Mehta is a children's author who believes that firing a child's imagination opens up a world of adventure. She has been writing for children for over two decades. She has authored the series *Discover India*—on the states of India; *Dealing with Feelings*—to help children deal with their own feelings; and *My Book of Values*—a series that helps inculcate values among young children. Her body of work is wide-ranging—she has created one of India's first dedicated children's newspaper sections; conceptualized the *Cadbury Bournvita Quiz Contest* for TV; and has written books, songs, poems and stories for leading publishers in India, several African nations, the USA and the UK.

She lives in Mumbai and runs Quadrum Solutions, a content company she co-founded. She is also the co-founder of PodSquad, a children's edutainment retail brand that firmly believes that children learn best when they are having fun.

Most days, Sonia can be found pounding away at her computer—when she is not playing with her dachshunds and her granddaughter, the three little loves of her life.

Read More in the Junior Lives Series

Mother Teresa
Mahatma Gandhi
Rani Lakshmibai
Gautama Buddha

Shivaji Maharaj

Sonia Mehta

Illustrated by Swapnil Behere

PUFFIN BOOKS

An imprint of Penguin Random House

PUFFIN BOOKS

USA | Canada | UK | Ireland | Australia
New Zealand | India | South Africa | China | Singapore

Puffin Books is part of the Penguin Random House group of companies
whose addresses can be found at global.penguinrandomhouse.com

Published by Penguin Random House India Pvt. Ltd
4th Floor, Capital Tower 1, MG Road,
Gurugram 122 002, Haryana, India

Penguin
Random House
India

First published in Puffin Books by Penguin Random House India 2018

Text and illustrations copyright © Quadrum Solutions Pvt. Ltd 2018
Series copyright © Penguin Random House India 2018

ISBN 9780143428282

Design and layout by Quadrum Solutions Pvt. Ltd
Printed at Manipal Technologies Limited, India

www.penguin.co.in

MIX
Paper | Supporting
responsible forestry
FSC® C043100

This is a legitimate digitally printed version of the book and therefore might not
have certain extra finishing on the cover.

Contents

Contents

1 Our Warrior Has Arrived

The baby boy looked around him curiously. Several grown-up faces peered down at him, some anxious, some amused. Outside, on the slopes of the Sahyadri mountain range, wolves howled and the branches of the trees creaked and sighed in the wind.

'Choose, my son,' the boy's mother urged. She had a quiet, calm strength about her, although her face showed that she was a little weary. 'It is time to choose your destiny,' she added.

The baby sat on a rough carpet woven with many bright images of objects—a pen, a sword, a scythe, a fishing boat and more. The grown-ups surrounding the baby believed that the object a baby reached for would reveal his or her destiny. Each object meant something different: a pen for a clerk, a scythe for a farmer and a sword for a warrior! The baby considered the images before him with keen eyes. Of all of them, the sword seemed to him the most attractive, and his plump little hand reached forward to trace its shape.

A cry of triumph arose from the watching group.

'Our warrior has arrived!' the people exclaimed, congratulating each other. The mother's eyes were wet with proud tears.

The baby was none other than Chhatrapati Shivaji Maharaj, the legendary warrior and the great king of the Marathas.

Who Were the Bhonsles?

Although he was born in the wilds of the Sahyadri range, Shivaji's family, the Bhonsles, weren't simple peasants. In fact, they were said to be the descendants of a royal Rajput family.

At this time in history, the Indian subcontinent was home to many kingdoms ruled by different kings. These kings often waged war on each other. Kingdoms frequently rose and fell. This meant that there was a constant need for good soldiers in their armies. Over the centuries, the Bhonsle men had become soldiers in various armies, offering their services to ruling kings for a sum of money.

Much before Shivaji was born, his grandfather, Maloji, had offered his services to the king of Ahmednagar. It was here that the Bhonsle family lived. The sultan of Ahmednagar honoured Maloji and rewarded him for his service with gifts of land in the western region of India. Thus Shivaji's grandfather and father, Shahaji, were part of the Ahmednagar army.

After some years serving the sultan, Shahaji decided it was time for him to leave and seek better opportunities elsewhere. Shahaji thought it would be a good idea to ally himself with a powerful kingdom. He gathered his

4

belongings and called his son Sambhaji (Shivaji's elder brother) to him. Then he travelled south to the kingdom of Bijapur, whose power and influence had been growing for some time.

His wife, Jijabai, was left alone, even though she was pregnant with their second child.

> ## Oh Really?
> There is a story that says Jijabai and Shahaji were just five years old when they were betrothed. In the story, their fathers made the match because both children got along well with each other. Imagine that!

But Jijabai was a strong woman. She decided to return to the family's ancestral lands in Maratha territory.

Born in the Wilderness

Jijabai made for Shivneri, a fort near modern-day Pune.

It was a lonely place, far out in the wilderness. The jungles around the fort were inhabited by wolves and other wild animals. Worse, they were filled with robbers and brigands who attacked travellers and the local villagers alike. The poor village folk quaked in their huts, never knowing when they would be attacked by beast or by man.

The fort had been abandoned by all save a few old servants. It was in this old and lonely place that Shivaji was born. With his father and brother away in the south, Shivaji was mainly raised by his strong and wise mother.

2 Growing Up

As he grew up, Shivaji spent a lot of
time exploring the wilderness
around the fort. Thanks to
all his childhood wandering,
Shivaji grew up knowing
every inch of his land. He
knew every secret pass, nook
and cranny, every rock,
every hill and every tree. He
knew the birds and beasts,
and the seasons in which they came and went.
He could climb a tree like a squirrel, hike up a
steep mountainside like a goat and scale walls like
a lizard. He could survive on just a single meal
a day and sleep just about anywhere. He didn't
know it then, but the lessons he learnt during
those hard times would stand him in good stead
in his later years.

'Come, sit with me and listen to stories of our ancestors,' Jijabai would tell Shivaji on cold, lonely, winter evenings. And he would sit with her and listen to stories about a time when there were no Mughals or sultans, and the Marathas were free to live their lives the way they wanted to.

It's True!
Jijabai was a very religious woman. During her isolation, she became even more so. She taught Shivaji to pray to God and to respect others.

'I will make sure we get our freedom and way of life back,' a young Shivaji thought to himself. 'I will unite my people and make us all proud to be Marathas again.'

THE STRENGTH OF THE MUGHALS

The Mughal Empire was spreading fast. When the Mughals defeated a kingdom, the defeated rulers had to submit to Mughal rule. This meant they had to pay taxes to the empire and provide soldiers. By the time Shivaji grew up, even the strongest of the Rajput kings, known for their immense bravery, had been defeated by the mighty Mughals.

A Family Reunion

Meanwhile, Shahaji had been doing very well in the Bijapur army and had become a nobleman in the sultan's court. He had married again and even had another son, named Vyankoji. His second wife was called Tukabai. Over the years, he had heard much about his younger son with Jijabai. People said he had grown up into a smart young man. Shahaji decided he wanted to meet Shivaji. And so, he sent for Jijabai and Shivaji, asking them to come to Bijapur.

It was a long journey to Bijapur. Shivaji, all of twelve years old, looked about him in awe as they rode into the city. The sultans of Bijapur were of Persian origin. The palaces with their grand domes and elaborate carvings seemed surreal to a boy brought up in an abandoned fort out in the wilderness. Merchants from Europe roamed the streets selling exotic wares like perfumes and silks. Magnificent camels and elephants walked along the roads, with nobles and royalty sitting atop them in their howdahs.

It was all very different from anything Shivaji had ever seen! Used to the rough ways of the hills, the young Maratha boy was tired of the pomp and show fast enough, finding it quite superficial and pointless. It only served to intensify his dislike for the Bijapuri way of life.

Refusing to Bow

Soon after the family was reunited, it was time for Shivaji to be presented to Sultan Mohammed Adil Shah. Shahaji proudly brought his son forth. He hoped that the sultan would take to Shivaji and give him a place in his court. But instead of bowing and scraping to the ruler, as was the custom in the court of Bijapur, Shivaji looked the sultan straight in the eye while bringing his palms together in a salutation that was traditional amongst his people.

Oh Wow!

Some historians think that the first sultan of Bijapur was a son of the Ottoman Emperor Murad II. Others think he may have been a slave who was brought to India by a Bahmani nobleman. Whatever his lineage, it was he who founded the Bijapur Sultanate, one of the richest Deccan kingdoms in India!

The sultan glared at the boy, and the entire court held its breath. This was a direct insult to the sultan and could result in Shivaji's or Shahaji's imprisonment or even death.

'Forgive him, your Majesty,' Shahaji leapt into action. He prostrated before the sultan. 'He doesn't know the ways of Bijapuri life. He has but just come from the hills.' His action saved the day and the sultan chose to overlook Shivaji's lack of humility.

Over the following months, Shivaji roamed the streets of Bijapur, observing the ways of this famous city. While his elder brother, Sambhaji, raised by his father, was more than willing to follow the rules and customs of Bijapur, Shivaji found the rules and regulations of court life stifling after the freedom of the hills. He got into trouble several times for disobeying the law of the land.

Finally, Shahaji gave up.

'I will never be able to make anything of you,' he said, disgusted. 'You had better go back home.'

Although Shivaji was sent back, Shahaji appointed a tutor named Dadoji Kondadev

15

to oversee his studies. Besides tutoring the young boy, Dadoji was also to oversee the family lands.

And at last, to Shivaji's great joy, he and his mother went back to their beloved hills. Shivaji was thirteen by this time.

3 A Guru and an Administrator

The home that Shivaji and Jijabai returned to was in shambles. Mughal troops had passed through on their way to Bijapur, ransacking villages, destroying fields and crops and ruining the tiny villages scattered throughout the region. Many villagers, with no fields to farm, had become

brigands, and lay in wait for trader caravans to pass by so they could rob them. Wolves, sensing the fear in the air, had become bolder, and it was dangerous for people to wander about alone.

Rebuilding a Land

'We must change things,' Dadoji, Shivaji's tutor told Jijabai when they returned. 'First, we must give the people employment, and a way to earn some money. I have an idea.'

The first thing to do was to tackle the wolf menace. Dadoji announced a handsome reward for every person who killed a wolf. The villagers and tribesmen found that they earned more by getting rid of the wild creatures than by looting caravans. Soon, the wolves had been wiped out, making the area safer. People also found they had money in their pockets, so there was no need to loot caravans.

Oh Really?
Jijabai did not have much money. So to make all this happen, it is said that Dadoji paid for everything with his own money.

Once that was done, Dadoji convinced the tribes to engage in farming and offered them land at very low rent. As more and more people picked up their shovels and hoes, the landscape changed. Wild hillsides gave way to lush farms, desperate robbers turned into hardworking farmers who reaped good harvests. Happy, secure and well-fed, people now began to build homes and temples.

Shivaji watched all this with great interest, filing away in his mind all the strategies he saw Dadoji use. This, too, was part of his education.

The Birth of Poona

One of the villages that lay on the Bhonsle land was called Poona (we now call it Pune). It had once been known for its lovely temples, but those had long been destroyed by rampaging troops.

'What an ideal spot to build a capital', Dadoji thought to himself. He set about rebuilding the village. With its location by a river and a wonderful climate, it was an attractive destination for a lot of people. Rich families who had abandoned the village and moved elsewhere in search of better opportunities returned to Poona. Soon, it became a bustling and prosperous town.

On the banks of the Muta river, Shahaji had built a magnificent mansion. It was called Lal Mahal (Red Palace).

Oh Really?

It is said that when Dadoji rebuilt Poona, he had it ploughed with white oxen pulling a plough made of pure gold! With this act, he aimed to get rid of any superstitions that people might be harbouring about returning to this wonderful land.

Dadoji established Shivaji and Jijabai in this lovely mansion.

Shivaji's Schooling

Finally, it was time for Dadoji to focus on Shivaji's education.

Every evening, by the flickering of oil lamps, Shivaji sat with Dadoji and listened to stories from the epics, spiritual poems written by great poet-saints and tales of the valour of heroes of old. These lessons with Dadoji left a lasting impression on Shivaji. All his life, he remained a deeply thoughtful person who respected all religions.

But this was just one part of Shivaji's education. Although he now lived in a grand mansion, he could not forget his beloved forests and hills that had been his home for so many years.

Shivaji spent his days engaged in intense exercise. He gathered around him a small band of men, who became his best friends. Along with them, he would scramble up every precarious hill, scale every cliff, explore every path and slither down every steep valley. Soon he knew every inch of his land like the back of his hand, with his faithful friends keeping pace.

Did You Know?
This small band of men went on to become the backbone of the fearsome Maratha army.

The villagers and forest-dwellers soon became familiar with this short but sturdy young man, who seemed to care about them and who knew no fear.

Every evening, Shivaji would come home and touch his mother's feet. Then he would have a simple meal of salted rice with buttermilk. He ended his day at the feet of his guru, engrossed in his studies.

Shivaji slowly grew to be a strong young man under the watchful eye of his wise tutor, Dadoji and his loving mother, Jijabai.

4 The First Rebellions

The years went by, and soon Shivaji grew to be a strapping young man of nineteen. As he went about his studies and exercise, he remained devoted to his mother. But not for a moment did he forget his ambition of bringing back the Maratha way of life.

The Rajputs in the north had accepted Mughal rule and were quite happy to marry off their princesses to Mughal princes. Even most Marathas were resigned to the fact that they would never have their own king. Dadoji himself felt that Shivaji's best option was to accept Mughal rule and find himself a high position at court. But Shivaji would have none of it.

'We must overthrow them. We must also find a way of beating the Bijapur troops,' he said. He was determined to carve out a land that the Marathas could call their own and could rule themselves.

Oh Really?

Shivaji's soldiers and followers sang songs called powadas. These are war or patriotic songs. Even now, these are very popular in Maharashtra. There are powadas about Shivaji's valour that people sing to this day.

Shivaji began to formulate a plan.

'For me to ever have any impact on the massive Mughal army, I will need weapons. And my poor men are hardly paid anything. I need to be able to pay them well and increase my army,' he thought, walking up and down, late into the night. Then he had an idea.

A Chain of Forts

It so happened that the Maratha lands were sandwiched between the Mughal and the Bijapur kingdoms. The two armies were frequently at war. On the frontier of Maratha land, there was a chain of forts that were occupied by Bijapur troops. It gave the sultan of Bijapur a line of defence against any approaching Mughal troops.

'This is where the troops keep their weapons,' thought Shivaji. 'These are the forts I must attack first.' He decided to focus on a fort called Torna.

A Clever Plan

Torna Fort stood on a hill at a great height, giving the troops a perfect view of the passes below that any army would have to cross if they wanted to go past it. The soldiers had to stay alert during summer and winter but the long, furious monsoons ensured that no one could pass by easily. The rainy season was a period of lull and the soldiers often got bored with nothing to do.

Shivaji waited and watched. The monsoon clouds gathered and torrential rains began. The commander of the troops based at the fort looked at his bored troops.

'I think they need a break,' he said to himself. 'I will give them permission to go to the plains for a week or so. No one will pass by or attack the fort in such terrible weather.' And so, all the troops

guarding Torna left and went down to the plains to have a good time.

This was the moment Shivaji had been waiting for. He and his band of followers slipped into the fort like mice. They quickly emptied the treasury and weapon room and made off with a great quantity of weapons and money. With the soldiers absent, they also managed to take control of the fort. The sultan of Bijapur was furious when he heard of this coup.

Now Shivaji's little army was stronger than before. But he was not yet content. There was more to be done.

Capturing the Lion Fort

His eye fell next on a fort called Sinhagad (Lion Fort). This was an important fort—larger, with more weapons and treasures, and in a critical strategic location. But looting this fort was as easy as pie for Shivaji, because now he had money.

He simply bribed the governor who was in charge and took over the fort without a single weapon being drawn.

Shivaji's treasury was growing richer. He had guns, weapons and more wealth than before. He was also in control of two major forts. It was time to look at other forts.

The Smartest Move

One of the largest forts in the area was Purandar Fort. Shivaji was desperate to capture it. But it was controlled by a cruel and shrewd governor. Shivaji waited and watched. Suddenly, news came that the governor had died. By law, it was expected that his son would take over. But the governor had three sons who were quarrelling over who would get to occupy the position.

Shivaji reached out and made an offer of friendship.

'I will be the mediator,' he offered, 'and help you out of this difficult situation.' The brothers, fed up of quarrelling, agreed. Knowing the influence Shivaji had in the land, they decided it would be a good idea to have him be part of the discussion. They invited him to the fort for a meeting.

What they didn't know was that for the past month or more, Shivaji's followers had been entering the fort dressed as coolies, carrying heavy bales of grass and wood. Concealed in these bales were weapons.

Shivaji made friends with the three brothers. One day, he suggested they go down to the plains to bathe in the clear streams.

'I know the best place to have a wonderful swim,' he told them. Sick of being stuck inside the fort, the brothers agreed. Soon the young men were having a good time splashing about. When it was time to return to the fort, they began walking up the ramparts.

Suddenly, the brothers stopped and stared. Instead of the flag of Bijapur, a Maratha flag flapped cheerfully atop the fort.

'What is this?' they yelled, rushing forward. They were stopped at the gates by rough-looking Maratha soldiers.

'Let us through,' they shouted.

'My friends,' Shivaji told them calmly. 'This fort now belongs to the Marathas.' The brothers looked aghast. They had been outwitted.

'Don't worry,' Shivaji consoled them. 'I will give you land and houses elsewhere. You can live there for the rest of your lives.'

And so, without shedding a single drop of blood, Shivaji had taken control of several important forts and made himself and his army stronger.

Life Goes On

By now Dadoji was an old man. He fell very ill. Shivaji, who loved Dadoji like a father, spent hours looking after him. He massaged his feet, bathed his forehead with cool water and sat by him for hours.

Dadoji had not been in favour of Shivaji's actions in taking the forts. But he knew that Shivaji was determined.

'Please forgive me, Dadoji,' Shivaji said. 'But I must bring glory to the Marathas again. I cannot do it without your blessing.' Dadoji smiled tiredly. And one evening, Dadoji blessed Shivaji, and died.

For many days, Shivaji was sad. Dadoji had been a strong influence in his life.

Around this time, Jijabai found a wife for Shivaji. Saibai was a simple, but a wise young woman. She had no ambitions of her own and was happy to stay in Shivaji's shadow.

Oh Really?

It's said that Saibai advised Shivaji and was a great companion to him. They were married nineteen years before she died of an illness. They had four children—three daughters and a son—Sakhubai, Ranubai, Ambikabai and Sambhaji.

5 Building an Army

Shivaji was getting stronger and more determined than ever to make his dream of a Maratha-ruled land a reality. He was armed with forts, and enough wealth to pay his soldiers. But his army was still nowhere near that of the mighty Mughals or the Sultanate of Bijapur.

I must continue to build my army', he thought. His eye fell upon a quiet little province that lay along the coast, near his land. The capital of this province was Kalyan. The province was under the protection of Bijapur. The governor, a man called Mulana Ahmed, was comfortably settled and too lazy to bother with trying to increase his territory.

A Surprise Raid

Many caravans of traders and merchants passed through this region. Mulana Ahmed allowed them to pass, and collected hefty sums of money from them. In turn, he had to send payment to the sultan of Bijapur.

One day, he sent off a large caravan with the entire year's payment—both in money and jewels—to be paid to the sultan. Shivaji's men lay in wait. As soon as they heard the creaking of the caravan wheels, they attacked the caravan and made off with the entire treasure.

The sultan was naturally very angry. He decided Shivaji must be taught a lesson.

'He has taken our forts, and now he is beginning to raid our caravans,' he thundered. 'Find him and kill him. At once!'

'Oh, Your Highness,' cried Shahaji, Shivaji's father, who was still loyal to the sultan. He fell at his feet. 'Please spare him.'

The sultan thought for a bit. He had heard how cunning Shivaji was and knew it would be difficult to capture him. He thought of an equally cunning plan.

'Imprison Shahaji!' he ordered his soldiers. 'Send a message to that mountain rascal that his father will be buried brick by brick unless he comes at once to court.'

The news of his father's imprisonment soon reached the ears of Shivaji. He had no great love for his father, but he was a dutiful son.

'If I go to the court of the sultan, I will surely be imprisoned,' he thought. 'I must think of another way to free my father.'

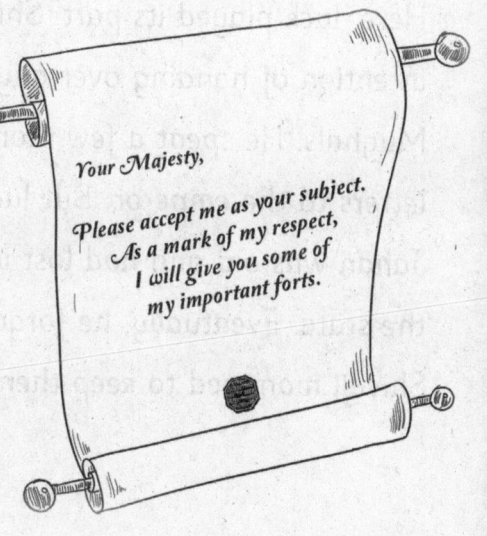

A Clever Idea

Shivaji sent a
flattering letter to
the Mughal emperor,
Shah Jahan.

Your Majesty,
Please accept me as your subject.
As a mark of my respect,
I will give you some of
my important forts.

When the emperor
received this letter,
he was pleased.

He sent a letter of acceptance to Shivaji. Not just that, he also sent a letter to the sultan, saying that Shivaji was now his subject.

When Shah Jahan's letter reached the sultan in Bijapur, he was stunned. And very worried too. If the emperor and Shivaji got together, there was no hope for Bijapur. He decided that being on Shivaji's bad side was not a good idea at all.

'Release Shahaji,' he ordered his soldiers quickly. And soon Shahaji was back home, safe and unharmed.

Here, luck played its part. Shivaji had no real intention of handing over any forts to the Mughals. He spent a few months writing flattering letters to the emperor. But luckily for him, Shah Jahan was old and had lost interest in affairs of the state. Eventually, he forgot about the forts and Shivaji managed to keep them.

HIRKANI

Shivaji spent a lot of time and effort on building strong forts. He wanted to make Raigad Fort, his capital, completely secure. He ordered the strongest, steepest walls to be built, so no one could ever climb them. One day, a peasant woman called Hirkani, who sold milk to the troops in the fort, got stuck in the fort, because it was evening and the gates were closed. She had a small baby at home and had to get out of the fort. When the guards refused to open the gates for her, she climbed down the steep walls and got home to her baby. Shivaji was so impressed, that he named a tower after her— the Hirkani Tower.

Spiritual Discoveries

Things were now peaceful for some time. This period is important because this was the time when Shivaji discovered two people whose thinking would come to influence him deeply.

He had heard of two poet-saints who wrote spiritual poetry. Their names were Sant Tukaram and Sant Ramdas.

Ramdas   Tukaram

When Shivaji first heard one of Tukaram's poems, he was so moved that he left home and wandered alone in the wilds of the Maratha plateau, looking for the man. He finally found Tukaram in an isolated hut. Shivaji donned the simple clothes

of a monk and sat
at Tukaram's feet.
He refused to go
back home, even
though his men
came to beg him to
return. Finally, the
men asked his mother
Jijabai to appeal to her son.

'You have built an army, and now you are
abandoning your men,' Jijabai told Shivaji, when
she went to meet him in Tukaram's hut. 'This is not
how a soldier behaves.'

Reluctantly, Shivaji went
back with his mother and
took charge of his troops
once more.

> **Did You Know?**
> Sant Tukaram's
> poetry is sung in
> temples even now.

A Message Arrives

Some time later, Sant Ramdas sent Shivaji a
poem along with gift of a handful of earth, some

pebbles and some horse dung. Shivaji's men were outraged.

'What kind of a gift is this to send to our king?' they fumed.

But Shivaji understood what it meant.

'Look further, my brothers,' he said. 'Sant Ramdas is sending me a message. The earth says I must conquer all the land; the pebbles are the forts that I must hold on to; and the horse dung is my cavalry of horses that will lead us to victory.'

That message seemed to bring Shivaji back to the task at hand. Soon, he was back on his horse, determined to fulfil his mission to make the Marathas great.

Oh Wow!
The followers of Sant Tukaram and Sant Ramdas always carried an ochre-coloured flag. Shivaji made his Maratha flag the same ochre.

6 The Mughals Take Action

Shah Jahan was an old man now. He had lost interest in his empire and spent more time grieving over his dead queen, Mumtaz (for whom he had built the Taj Mahal) than on governing his lands. It was the perfect time for his youngest son Aurangzeb to act.

Did You Know?

Shah Jahan lived for eight years as a prisoner in Agra Fort. His room had a tiny window from which he could see the Taj Mahal, and remember his beloved queen Mumtaz.

A Man of Ambition

Aurangzeb was as ruthless as he was ambitious and cunning. He had two older brothers. They had better claims to the throne. But, without a second thought, he had them killed. He imprisoned his father Shah Jahan in Agra Fort, along with his sister, Jahanara. And finally, he declared himself emperor.

Oh Really?

Aurangzeb rose at the crack of dawn, and bathed and prayed. He was a vegetarian and ate hardly anything. He slept for barely two hours every night and spent the rest of his night reading the Koran.

Even before Aurangzeb became emperor, his advisors had warned him about Shivaji.

'Your Highness, it would be good to keep an eye on this man,' they warned him.

'Ah, bah! We don't have the time to waste on some small, useless piece of land ruled by a hill chief,' Aurangzeb scoffed. 'We have better things to do.' He had his eye on the rich sultanate of Bijapur. He wanted to crush it.

Attack!

Aurangzeb decided to attack. He set forth with a massive army—complete with hundreds of elephants and thousands of horses and men. Shivaji watched this with great interest. He was itching to get involved, but he knew his own army was much too small to take on the strength of the Mughal army.

'But that doesn't stop me from taking advantage of their distraction,' he thought gleefully.

He waited until the bulk of the army had passed by and then, along with a few hundred soldiers, he attacked Ahmednagar. Many of Aurangzeb's horses were being rested here. Shivaji made off with more than a thousand of them.

Aurangzeb was furious. He began plotting his vengeance. But luckily for Shivaji, Aurangzeb had to return to his capital, because his father, Shah Jahan was seriously ill and was expected to die. He rushed immediately to Agra, and postponed his revenge on Shivaji.

The sultan of Bijapur was a relieved man because Aurangzeb had to abandon his attack on Bijapur.

But, as it happened, he didn't live long enough to enjoy his relief. He died soon after, and the queen mother, Taaj Sultana, a strong woman, decided to take matters into her own hands.

The Tale of Afzal Khan

'We must take revenge on that mountain rascal Shivaji for the way in which he stole our forts,' she thought. She called upon Afzal Khan, an Afghan warrior and commander in the Bijapur army. He was known to be powerful and cruel.

'Go and kill Shivaji,' she ordered him. Afzal Khan set forth with his army. He ruthlessly killed anyone who came in his way. As he approached Maratha territory, the villagers' terror began to grow. 'The Bijapur army is attacking us,' was the rumour that flew around. When Shivaji heard this, he was quite unperturbed. When Afzal Khan was closer, he sent messengers to invite him to dine.

Thinking this was just the gesture of a weak man, Afzal Khan accepted. He was delighted because he thought he could now kill Shivaji in his own home. But he didn't know that Shivaji, as usual, had a clever plan up his sleeve.

The Killer Embrace

Unknown to anyone, Shivaji had acquired a set of sharp steel claws that he hid in his clothes. When Afzal Khan approached him, Shivaji rose to greet him in an embrace. Afzal Khan was tall like a giant, while Shivaji was a short man, hardly reaching Afzal Khan's shoulders.

'This is too easy,' the big man laughed to himself. 'I can strangle this dwarf with my bare hands.' As the men embraced, Shivaji dug the talons deep into Afzal Khan's back. Afzal Khan fell dead with a cry. Before his men could come to save their master, Shivaji's guards had overcome them. Shivaji had sent an army to attack Afzal Khan's camps. Not expecting a Maratha attack, the Bijapuri troops were easily overcome.

Shivaji had triumphed once more.

Oh Really?

Shivaji was known to be generous towards his enemies once they had surrendered. He spared the lives of many of Afzal Khan's soldiers and even sent them home with small gifts and money.

7 Clever Tactics

By now, with his father dead, Aurangzeb was firmly established as the Mughal emperor. But he hadn't forgotten how Shivaji had taken a thousand horses from him.

'We had better crush this mountain rat before he causes any more trouble,' he told his commanders. He asked his uncle, a strong and clever man called Shaista Khan to go south and defeat Shivaji.

Shaista Khan's Attack

And so, the mighty Shaista Khan set forth with a cavalry of hundred thousand horses, massive artillery and a full regiment of Pathan soldiers. Shivaji's tiny army was no match for this mighty force, so he prudently retreated. But by no means had he given up! He was simply biding his time and formulating one of his famous plans.

Shaista Khan marched triumphantly into Poona. The Mughal army occupied the whole of the city. They closed the gates of the city at night to any Maratha—soldier or civilian. The Maratha people who were not a part of the army, were only allowed to enter the city during the day. Shaista Khan himself stayed in Lal Mahal, Shivaji and Jijabai's home, which they had been forced to abandon.

Then the monsoon broke. The troops had to halt for they were not used to such heavy rain. The entire army stayed put within the walls of Poona.

One day, one of the guards received a request.

'A wedding party wishes to enter the city to carry out one of their customs,' he explained to Shaista Khan. 'Should I give them permission?'

'Oh, what can a stupid wedding party do?' Shaista Khan said irritably. He was getting impatient. 'Let them in. And apply your mind to how we can get rid of that pesky Shivaji.'

Outwitted Again

And so, the wedding procession came through the gates. The bridegroom, his face covered with flowers, rode a horse right in front. Around him were common people dressed in wedding finery.

Just behind the wedding procession came a troop of Mughal horsemen. They herded before them some Maratha soldiers who they had captured and were beating them mercilessly.

The Mughal guards laughed as they passed through.

Night fell. In a remote corner, unknown to the Mughal soldiers on guard, the wedding party, the Mughal horsemen and the Maratha prisoners all threw off their disguises. They were all Shivaji's men, and Shivaji himself was among them.

Like shadows, Shivaji and his men crept along the dark walls and entered Lal Mahal.

The Slash of The Dagger

Shaista Khan was fast asleep in Shivaji's own chamber. Shivaji leapt on him and slashed at him with his dagger. Shaista Khan rolled over and let out a roar that could be heard all through the palace. Shivaji missed his heart, but Shaista Khan's thumb was neatly sliced off.

As soon as Shaista Khan bellowed, his guards, who were relaxing in the dead of night, sprang into action. But Shivaji's men had occupied the palace and soon quelled them.

As Shaista Khan rode out on an elephant to get away, a battle followed. The Mughals, although far stronger and with greater numbers, were totally unprepared. Finally, Shaista Khan gave the order to evacuate Poona and return to Delhi.

Once more, Shivaji had outwitted the Mughals.

Aurangzeb was furious. But he was preoccupied. His favourite sister, Roshanara, had wanted to see Kashmir and he was on his way to Kashmir with an enormous entourage. He decided to deal with Shivaji on his return from Kashmir.

But Shivaji wasn't going to wait around for this. He was keen paying the Mughals back for the fiasco in Poona. But instead of attacking with an army, he attacked with an idea.

The Wealth of Surat

The city of Surat was a major trading centre. Arab, Chinese, Dutch, French and Portuguese traders, bought and sold their valuable merchandise here. The British, who had entered India as traders, had weapons factories here. Surat was possibly one of the richest cities in India at the time. And this was what Shivaji set his eyes on.

As it happened, the governor of Surat was known to be a man who took it easy and liked to enjoy the good things in life. As long as he paid his taxes to the Mughal court, he was free to live in luxury, surrounded by food, music and drink. The citizens were so intent on making money that they had no idea that Shivaji, with a cavalry of 4,000, was camped on the outskirts of Surat.

By the time the news reached the Mughal troops stationed in Surat, it was too late. Shivaji's men had entered Surat and taken away huge amounts of wealth.

Oh Really?

Shivaji, dressed as a beggar, entered Surat to study what kind of defences they had. This way, he found out for himself what wealth lay where, and what kind of guards there were in Surat.

This was the last straw. Aurangzeb was livid.

'This cannot continue. We cannot allow Shivaji to get away this time,' he roared.

8 The Wrath of Aurangzeb

Slowly but surely, Shivaji was gaining power. He didn't fight giant battles. But he was known for quick, unexpected lightning strikes and sudden, clever manoeuvres. He understood the importance of a navy. He built small, crude ships, which weren't great battle ships, but which troubled Mughal trading ships as they plundered their wealth.

Finally, Aurangzeb

could stand it no more. He called upon a Rajput king called Raja Jai Singh, who fought in the Mughal army.

'People tell me that you are a fearless warrior and a great leader. Well, prove it to me then. Capture this pest they call Shivaji. And destroy the Marathas, once and for all,' Emporer Aurangzeb commanded Jai Singh.

A Shrewd Enemy

Jai Singh was indeed a brave soldier. Like many Rajput kings, he had accepted Aurangzeb's might and now fought in the Mughal army.

Jai Singh learnt from the mistakes of those who had gone before him. He didn't underestimate Shivaji. He set about making plans for Shivaji's capture. For the first time, Shivaji had an enemy who was as cunning and clever as he was. Jai Singh didn't just march grandly into attack. He laid careful plans.

He convinced the Bijapur army to fight to regain their lost forts. He persuaded the Mughal traders to support him by reminding them how Shivaji's ships attacked them and disrupted trade. And finally, he made his own plans.

'Shivaji's strengths are his forts,' he mused. 'We shall attack one of the largest.' So he launched an attack on the fearsome Purandar Fort.

A Fierce Battle

Shivaji had a thousand soldiers guarding Purandar Fort. But Jai Singh attacked with twenty thousand soldiers. He had more guns, more horses and elephants. A fierce battle followed in which both sides lost many soldiers.

Jai Singh also sent his troops to Raigad Fort, where Shivaji's family lived. Shivaji realized that continuing to fight was foolhardy.

'Let us arrive at a solution,' he wrote in a letter to Jai Singh.

But Jai Singh would not hear of any compromise. He wanted Shivaji to surrender to him.

Finally, when Shivaji saw his beloved Purandar Fort being mercilessly attacked, he agreed to meet Jai Singh. When Shivaji walked into Jai Singh's tent, the Rajput embraced him warmly. He treated him with great respect and affection. For he, like Shivaji, was an honourable man and held Shivaji in the greatest esteem.

Shivaji agreed to give twenty-three forts to Aurangzeb, and agreed to live as a subject of the Mughal Empire.

'Shivaji is a great soldier and a fair man,' Jai Singh wrote in a letter to Aurangzeb. 'Pardon him and you will have a loyal ally for life.' Jai Singh respected Shivaji and didn't want any harm to come to him.

A Suspicious Letter

Aurangzeb wasn't happy. Even though Shivaji had surrendered his forts, and accepted defeat, Aurangzeb wanted Shivaji himself.

'This time, I will take matters into my own hands,' he decided. He wrote a very polite letter to Shivaji.

'We have heard much about your bravery. We would like to meet you. Come to our court, and we promise you will be safe.' The letter was flowery and warm. It made Shivaji suspicious.

'I think I will go and meet this Aurangzeb once and for all,' Shivaji decided. He went off to the Mughal court with Sambhaji, his ten-year-old son.

The Mughal court was in Agra. The noblemen lived in luxurious houses here. Shivaji was given a mansion called Jaipur House. Agra was full of wonderful buildings, palaces, mosques and mansions. Luxury was everywhere. After three days, Shivaji was summoned to meet Aurangzeb at the durbar.

But instead of being seated amongst noblemen, Shivaji was given a seat right at the back, with common soldiers.

'Hmm. I can see he plans to insult me,' Shivaji thought to himself. But he decided to remain quiet and see what came next.

Oh Really?

When Shivaji was presented to Aurangzeb, instead of greeting him in the Mughal style, Shivaji merely saluted him in the way he was saluted by his people. The court was stunned. But Aurangzeb merely nodded. He had a plan.

That evening, when Shivaji returned to Jaipur House, the house was suddenly surrounded by Mughal soldiers.

'You are a prisoner now,' the main guard told Shivaji. 'Neither you nor your son may leave this building.'

Trapped

Shivaji was well and truly trapped. There was no way out. But instead of being dismayed, he began to plan.

'Now Aurangzeb has had it,' he thought fiercely. 'Imprisoning my son and me through trickery is not what kings and emperors should do. I will escape and then teach him a lesson.'

He stayed calm and behaved as though he accepted his imprisonment. Aurangzeb kept an eye on him through his guards.

'Your Highness, Shivaji seems quite content to be a prisoner,' they reported. 'He eats, sleeps and even sends gifts of fruit and food cooked in the Maratha way to Mughal noblemen.'

'Hah! We knew it! That brave mountain lion is actually a cowardly rabbit,' scoffed Aurangzeb scornfully. 'Keep an eye on him. And one of these days, we shall get rid of him forever.'

Tricked Once More

Shivaji made it a custom to send massive baskets of fruit and food to noblemen. In the beginning, the guards would open each basket and check inside. But after three months of doing this, they got bored.

'Bah, it is just as the emperor said,' they muttered to each other. 'This man is a coward.'

One day, as usual, a procession of baskets

Oh Really?

Aurangzeb didn't know it, but Shivaji had one ally in his court and that was his daughter Zinat-un-Nisa. It is said that she fell in love with Shivaji's bravery. Many years later, after Shivaji was dead, she looked after his grandson, also named Shivaji, who was brought to the Mughal court.

passed through the gates of the mansion. They looked exactly the same as they had every day.

'Let them through,' the guards said, lazily waving them on.

The procession of baskets was taken through the market and right into the jungles. Once they were a safe distance from the city, out of the baskets came Shivaji and his young son Sambhaji. Disguised sometimes as a beggar, sometimes as a monk, Shivaji made his way back home.

One evening, a while later, Jijabai was praying in her room. A beggar, dressed in rags his face covered with a rough shawl, was brought to her.

'What do you want?' she asked the beggar kindly.

'To be at your feet,' the beggar replied, throwing off his shawl. It was Shivaji, home at last.

Once again, Shivaji had outwitted his enemies.

9 Getting Back His Forts

Back in his lands, Shivaji took back the reins from his mother Jijabai, who had been managing things in his absence.

Aurangzeb was furious that Shivaji had got away, but he was helpless.

'Your Highness, we must sign a treaty with Shivaji,' his advisors told him. 'He was dangerous before, but now he will be even more so. It's better to have him as an ally rather than an enemy.'

Reluctantly, the Mughals had to sign a new treaty with Shivaji in which they returned most of the forts they had grabbed. But they still held on to the strongest of them all—Purandar Fort and Sinhagad Fort.

> **Oh Really?**
> Shivaji is said to have had three favourite swords. He even gave them names—Bhawani, Jagdamba and Tulja.

One early morning, Jijabai was sitting at her window in Raigad Fort. The sun rose and glinted on the stone walls of Sinhagad Fort in the distance, which had a Mughal flag fluttering on it. She looked wistfully at the fort, once the object of Maratha pride and joy.

'Send for my son,' she ordered her messengers.

A short while later, Shivaji rode up.

'Mother, you sent for me?' he asked her, after touching her feet.

'I was lonely. I thought we could play a game of dice,' she said smiling.

'Of course,' Shivaji agreed at once. His mother was his world and he would do anything for her.

They played several rounds of dice and Jijabai won every game.

'You are the victor,' Shivaji said finally. 'What payment would you like from me?'

Jijabai looked at him for a moment and then looked at the window where the evening sun was making Sinhagad Fort glow.

'I want my fort back,' she said simply.

For Shivaji, his mother's word was law. It was going to be a tough battle, but once he decided, nothing could stop him.

He called on his most loyal and trusted commander, Tanaji Malusare.

'Go, my brother. Our mother wishes for Sinhagad. Get it back for her,' he told Tanaji.

A Mighty Battle

Tanaji didn't hesitate for a minute. Though he knew it was going to be a near impossible task, he was going to do it—or die trying.

The walls of Sinhagad Fort were steep and impossible to climb. Tanaji had a giant pet iguana, known as a ghorpad in the local language. This iguana was

extraordinarily large, almost like a little
dinosaur. Its name was Yeshwant.

Tanaji tied a strong rope
around Yeshwant's neck
and sent it up the
steep walls of the
fort. The iguana
ran up nimbly and
disappeared into
the fort.

Very quickly, Tanaji
and his soldiers
climbed up the rope and entered the fort stealthily.
Soon, an army of Maratha soldiers had taken the
Mughal troops completely by surprise. A massive
battle followed.

Tanaji was struck and fell to the ground, fatally
wounded. But his soldiers had overcome the
Mughal troops. As he lay dying, Tanaji ordered a
mighty flame to be lit.

Shivaji saw Sinhagad blaze with a brilliant light. It was the sign he had agreed on with Tanaji, which told him that victory was theirs.

'The Lion Fort is yours again,' Shivaji told his mother.

When his wounded and battle-scarred soldiers brought Tanaji's body back, Shivaji wept.

'I have won the Lion Fort, but I have lost my lion,' he said sorrowfully.

10 King at Last

Over the next several years, Shivaji grew stronger and stronger. He conquered a large part of the south of the subcontinent. He attacked Surat many times and added greatly to the wealth of his treasury.

Around this time, depressed by the way Shivaji was constantly ahead of him, Aurangzeb's army too had lost interest in doing battle with Shivaji's troops. They became lazy. When the sultan of Bijapur died, Shivaji was able to take part of Bijapur too!

Soon, Shivaji and his Maratha kingdom became a strong force.

The Coronation

Shivaji decided to crown himself king. Even though his people already thought of him as king, and even called him Maharaj (meaning Highness), he had never been properly crowned.

A grand ceremony was held and Shivaji, with his second wife, Soyrabai, beside him, became the official king of a large part of the Indian subcontinent.

Did You Know?
Shivaji was given the title chhatrapati, meaning monarch. So Shivaji became Chhatrapati Shivaji Maharaj.

A few years after his coronation, his mother Jijabai, who was quite old by then, died peacefully. Shivaji was devastated. He had loved his mother above all else in the world. He was sad over her passing for many months. He lost interest in everything. He began to fall ill a lot.

One Last Battle

But he still had one last fight in him. When he recovered, he decided to attack and take over the Carnatic region, a region that today is occupied by parts of Andhra Pradesh, Tamil Nadu and Karnataka.

To reach the Carnatic, he had to go through the rich kingdom of Golconda. He made friends with the ruler of Golconda, Abu Hussein, and asked for permission for his troops to pass through. He even made a deal with Abu Hussein.

'I will come to your aid if the Mughals ever attack you.

But in return, you must give me the use of your artillery and wealth,' he said. It was a good deal.

Shivaji marched on towards the Carnatic. A mighty battle was fought and Shivaji's army was victorious.

Trouble at Home

When a victorious Shivaji returned home after, he found his household in trouble.

His wife Soyrabai, an ambitious woman, wanted her son Rajaram to become king after Shivaji, and not his other son Sambhaji, who was Saibai's son.

She put pressure on Shivaji to favour her son.

'You know that Rajaram is more capable,' she argued. 'So what if he is not your oldest son?'

Shivaji tried to reason with her. But finally, he grew tired.

'I am tired of this palace life. I want to meditate and pray,' he wrote to Sant Ramdas, the poet-saint who had fascinated him years ago. 'I wish god would take me and reunite me with my mother.'

The End Is Near

It was almost as if he knew what was coming. In 1680, he fell seriously ill. A painful swelling in his knee became worse. Soon he fell into a deep fever, from which he never recovered. Finally, at the age of fifty, he breathed his last.

His loyal followers took his precious sword and placed it in the temple of the Goddess Saraswati at a place called Satara, where it remains today.

When Aurangzeb heard this news, he reacted in an unexpected way.

'He was a great soldier,' he said, 'and a worthy enemy.'

The era of Shivaji had come to an end. He is the only king in Indian history to take on the mighty Mughals and win.

Even today, more than 300 years later, his loyal followers sing songs of his bravery and tell stories of his conquests.

11 Timeline

1630   Shivaji is born to Jijabai and Shahaji.

1643–47   Shivaji occupies key forts.

1647   Shivaji's guardian Dadoji Kondadev dies.

1657   Shivaji's first encounter with the Mughals when he raids Ahmednagar.

1659   Afzal Khan is killed by Shivaji.

1660   Shaista Khan occupies Pune.

1663   Shivaji attacks Shaista Khan and cuts off his thumb.

1664   Shivaji's first raid on Surat.

1665   Jai Singh takes Purandar Fort and forces Shivaji to sign the treaty of Purandar.

1666   Shivaji escapes from Agra in a basket.

1674   Shivaji crowns himself king and takes on the title of Maharaja Chhatrapati.

1674   Jijabai dies.

1676   Shivaji's last battle in the Carnatic.

1680   Shivaji dies.

12 And Then What Happened?

What happened to all the people who had been a part of Shivaji's life after his death? What did Aurangzeb do after he lost his greatest enemy? And where did Shivaji's wife and children go?

Aurangzeb

Aurangzeb had fought Shivaji almost all his life as emperor. Finally, with Shivaji gone, he tried to expand his empire. But he was very unpopular, because of his spartan ways. Slowly, people began to revolt. The Rajput kings were fed up of his ways. The Jats revolted and the Marathas, even after Shivaji, continued to fight Aurangzeb.

Finally, Aurangzeb fell ill and died at the age of eighty-nine in 1707. Most of his children had died before him. His son, Bahadur Shah, who became emperor after Aurangzeb, was a weak king and poor leader. Over the years, Mughal power declined and soon their great empire was reduced to nothing more than a small kingdom around Delhi.

When Aurangzeb died, he said to his son, Azam, 'I came alone into this world. And now I am going as a stranger. I have done many unforgivable things. I have sinned and don't know if god will forgive me.'

Sambhaji

After Shivaji died, Sambhaji became king. He wasn't popular like his father was. And nor was he a wise ruler. He imprisoned his half-brother Rajaram and his step-mother Soyrabai.

He fought many battles, though not as successfully as his father.

Finally, in a fierce battle with the Mughals, he was captured. Aurangzeb had him put to death.

Shivaji's wives

As we saw, it wasn't against the law for a man to have more than one wife at this time in history. Shivaji had four wives. Shivaji's first wife, Saibai Nimbalker, was the mother of Sambhaji. She died some years after giving birth to him. She was a simple woman. They had four children—three daughters and one son.

Soyrabai Mohite, his second wife, was the mother of Rajaram. Soyrabai was an ambitious woman, who fought long and hard for her son to become king after Shivaji. It is said she tried to poison

Sambhaji because that's how much she resented him! Eventually, the story goes, it was Sambhaji who had her killed.

Putlabai Palkar was a devoted wife. She never had any children. It's said that she died immediately after Shivaji as she could not bear to live without him.

Oh Really?

There are some who say Shivaji had seven or eight wives. But there is no historical certainty about this claim.

Sakwar Bai Gaikwad, Shivaji's fourth wife, had one daughter. Some years after Shivaji's death, she was captured by Mughal troops and held prisoner till her death.

The Marathas after Shivaji

Shivaji left behind an empire that was always at loggerheads with the Mughals. With Shivaji no longer there to outwit him, Aurangzeb attacked the south, wanting to take over all the territory ruled by the Marathas. He captured Sambhaji and tortured him to death. Sambhaji's half-brother,

Rajaram became king, and after his death, his widow, Tarabai took over. There were many battles with the Mughals, but finally the Marathas defeated them.

Shahu, Shivaji's grandson (Sambhaji's son), ruled for some years. He appointed a man called Balaji Viswanath, a Peshwa. With that, began the era of Peshwa power.

The Peshwas, particularly Peshwa Balaji Bajirao, were great military leaders. At its peak, the Maratha Empire stretched all the way from Tamil Nadu to Peshawar (now in Pakistan).

Over the years, after fighting and losing many battles, the Maratha Empire began to slowly decline. Shahu Maharaj and the Peshwas allowed smaller chiefs to manage bits of the Maratha Empire. Families like the Gaekwads, the Holkars and the Scindias began to manage territories.

The British were getting stronger and finally defeated the Marathas—bringing to an end a glorious era.

13 Bibliography

Cousens, Henry. *Bijapur: The Old Capital of the Adil Shahi Kings*. India, 1889. http://www.rarebooksocietyofindia.org/book_archive/196174216674_10153275717891675.pdf

Farooqui, Salma. *A Comprehensive History of Medieval India from the Twelfth to the Mid-Eighteenth Century*. New Delhi: Dorling Kindersley India, 2011.

Indhistory. 'Shivaji Maharaj.' http://www.indhistory.com/shivaji.html

Kincaid, Dennis. *Shivaji: The Grand Rebel*. New Delhi: Rupa Publications, 2015.

MapsofIndia.com. 'Chhatrapati Shivaji Biography.' https://www.mapsofindia.com/who-is-who/history/chatrapati-shivaji.html

Shodhganga: Indian Electronic Theses and Dissertations. 'Chapter III: Fall of Bijapur.' http://shodhganga.inflibnet.ac.in/bitstream/10603/140673/9/09_chapter%203.pdf

SSC History. Editorial Board High Speed Publication, 2018.